JEWEL STICKER STORIES

Ten Little
Ballerinas

By Wendy Cheyette Lewison

Illustrated by Joan Holub

Grosset & Dunlap • New York

Copyright © 1996 by Grosset & Dunlap, Inc. Illustrations copyright © 1996 by Joan Holub. All rights reserved. Published by Grosset & Dunlap, Inc., a member of Penguin Putnam Books for Young Readers, New York. GROSSET & DUNLAP is a trademark of Grosset & Dunlap, Inc. Published simultaneously in Canada. Printed in the U.S.A.

ISBN 0-448-41491-0   2004 Printing

One ballerina loves to dance,
But what is she to do?
She's danced and danced
And danced and danced,
And now she's lost her shoe!

**Can you help her find the shoe?
Put a sticker on it.**

One ballerina goes up and down.
She's doing a plié.
But where is the bow that she wore
In dancing class today?

Can you find the
bow for her?
Put a sticker on it.

One ballerina twirls around.
She doesn't seem to see
The tiny kitten watching her
Behind the apple tree.

Do YOU see the kitten?
Put a sticker on her collar.

One ballerina leaps so far,
She leaps right out the door!
But where's her pretty necklace?
It fell down on the floor!

Can you find the necklace?
Put a sticker on it.

One ballerina, on her toes,
Has lost her fancy fan.
She cannot find it anywhere.
Do you think you can?

Can you find the fancy fan?
Put a sticker on it.

One ballerina all alone,
Having toast and tea.
She'd like her cuddly teddy bear
To keep her company.

Can you find the teddy bear?
Put a sticker on him.

One ballerina likes to paint.
She wants her doll to see
The picture that she's made of her.
Where could that dolly be?

Find the doll and
put a sticker on her.

One ballerina in the dressing room,
Brushing her long, long hair.
Ten pink tutus hang on hooks.
Which one should she wear?

**Pick out your favorite tutu.
Put a sticker on it.**

One ballerina, sad and blue,
Wears an unhappy frown.
She's looking here and everywhere,
But she cannot find her crown.

Make the ballerina smile.
Find her crown and
put a sticker on it.

One ballerina all dressed up.
Doesn't she look cute!
The musicians are ready to play for her,
But one can't find his flute.

Can you find the flute for him?
Put a sticker on it.

Ten ballerinas on the stage,
Making a graceful bow.
Each one will get a pretty rose,
But who has the roses now?

Can you find out who?
Put a sticker on each rose.

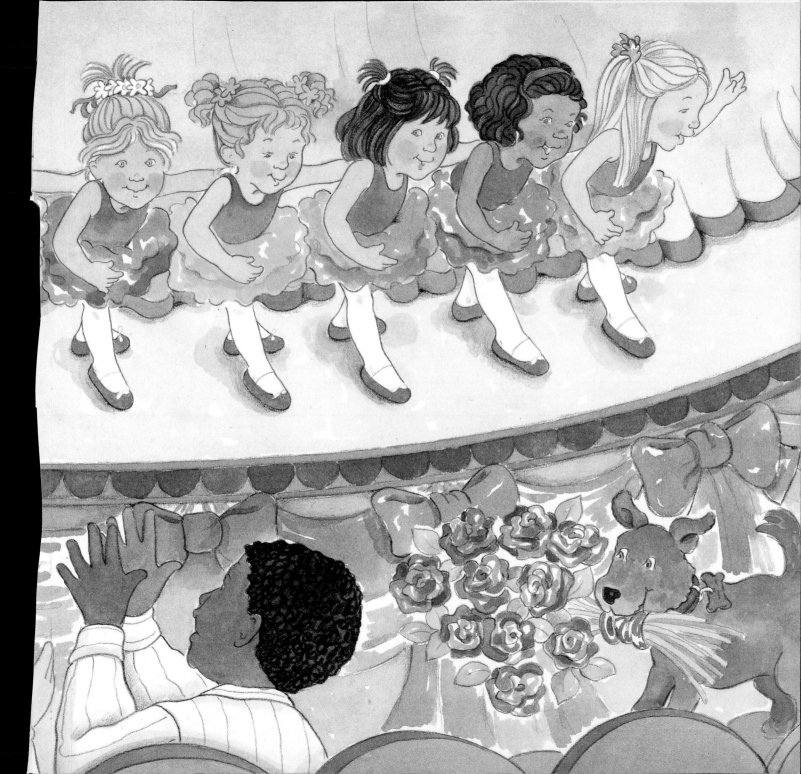

Ten ballerinas, ten sleepyheads,
Fall down in a heap.
Their dancing day is over now,
And they are fast asleep.

Shh-h-h.